For all animals, and the people
who love them x – B. D.

For small and big friends – C. B.

tiger tales
5 River Road, Suite 128, Wilton, CT 06897
Published in the United States 2021
Text by Becky Davies
Text copyright © 2021 Little Tiger Press Ltd.
Illustrations copyright © 2021 Charlotte Bruijn
ISBN-13: 978-1-68010-242-0 • ISBN-10: 1-68010-242-7
Printed in China • LTP/2800/3511/1220

www.tigertalesbooks.com

YOU CAN BE A FARMER, TOO!

by Becky Davies   Illustrated by Charlotte Bruijn

tiger tales

Emily loved helping Uncle Ben on the farm.
It was **messy**, **loud**, and *fun!*

Noah wasn't so sure. To him it was **messy**, **loud**, and **scary**.
The chickens had sharp beaks and claws.

The pigs were **enormous**.
But **scariest** of all was the cow.

"She won't hurt you, Noah,"
said Uncle Ben. "Just be gentle!"

But Noah
was still afraid.

"Being a farmer is fun," said Emily. "You'll enjoy it when you try, Noah. Watch me!"

They were kind of . . . cute.

"Wait for me!" Noah cried. He was beginning to enjoy himself.
Being a farmer **still** seemed messy . . . .

We can **dig** with the pig!

And it was definitely loud . . . .

Quack like Duck, twice for luck.

Clear your throat . . . bleat with Goat.

But it was also **a lot** of fun.

First, of course, brush the horse.

Next is Hen. Sweep her pen.

See that chick? Feed him, quick!

Play with Cat. Yes, like that.

home sweet home

Build a house for the mouse.

We can dig with the pig!

Quack!

Quack like Duck, twice for luck.

Bleat!

Clear your throat . . . bleat with Goat.

Jump and **leap** with lambs and sheep!

Ready?

Ready!

Mooooooooo

"I did it, I did it!" giggled Noah.

"Now there's just one more thing to do," said Emily.

"Turn around and close your eyes . . . ."

"I'm a farmer!" said Noah.
"That's right," laughed Emily.
"A **real** farmer!"